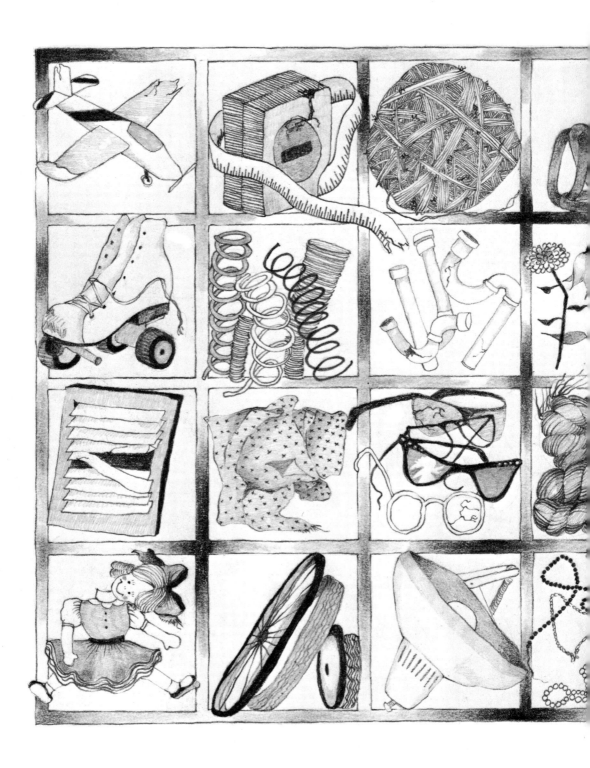

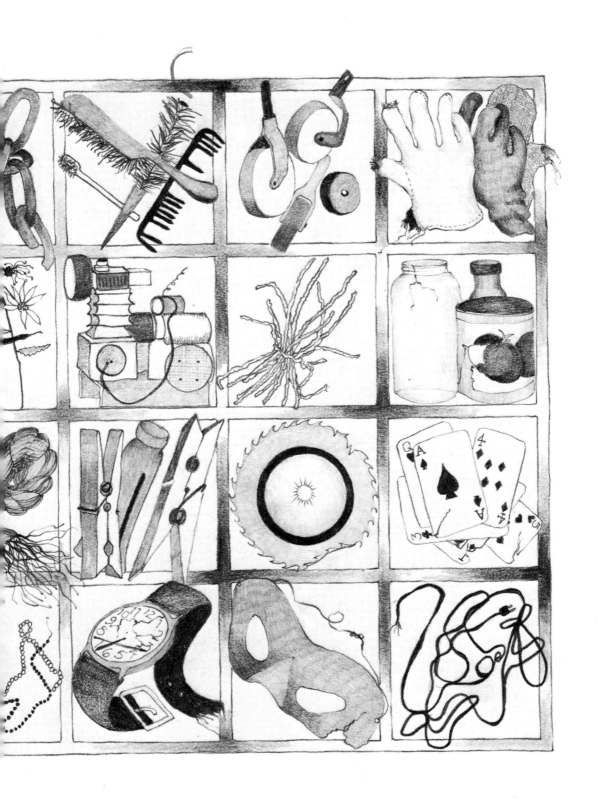

# Joe's Junk

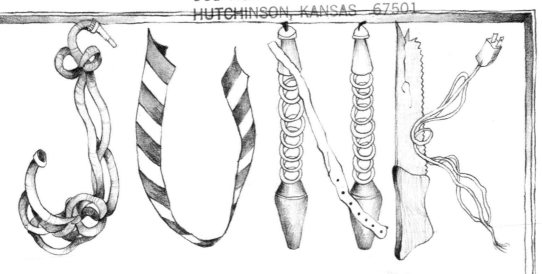

# by Susan Russo

## Holt, Rinehart and Winston / New York

**Library of Congress Cataloging in Publication Data**

Russo, Susan.
   Joe's junk.

   Summary: When his room begins to have a funny smell and
he has a hard time finding things, Joe's parents insist on
a garage sale to dispose of the junk Joe has collected.
   [1. Collectors and collecting—Fiction.   2. Cleanliness—
Fiction.   3. Garage sales—Fiction]   I. Title.
PZ7.R9193Jo   [Fic]   81-13228
ISBN 0-03-061264-0   AACR2

ISBN 0-03-061264

For my Joe, Alex

My name is Joe. All my life I've been a collector. Not of normal stuff like rocks or insects. I'm famous for my spectacular collection of junk.

"You trash it and I'll stash it!" That's my motto.

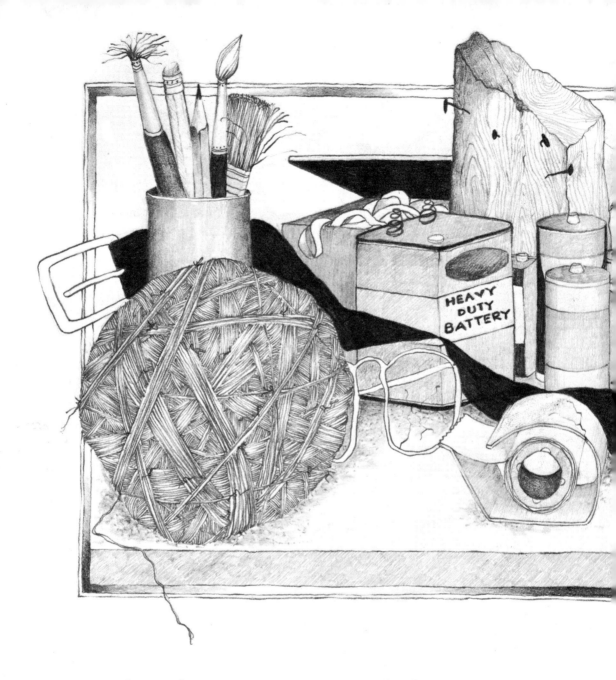

I am also a great inventor. Besides being crammed with junk, my room is a laboratory. I have a huge box of wire and some old bicycle parts. I have a ball of used

string you wouldn't believe, two *enormous* jars of nuts and bolts and seventeen used batteries. And that's only the beginning.

Naturally, my room is my favorite place.

But Mother sighs when she walks by my room. My father shudders and says, "Unfit for human habitation," whatever *that* means.

I have made some really incredible inventions with my junk. A plane I made looked a little strange, but it *almost* took off from the living-room rug. My mother was a good sport when it collided with her favorite lamp.

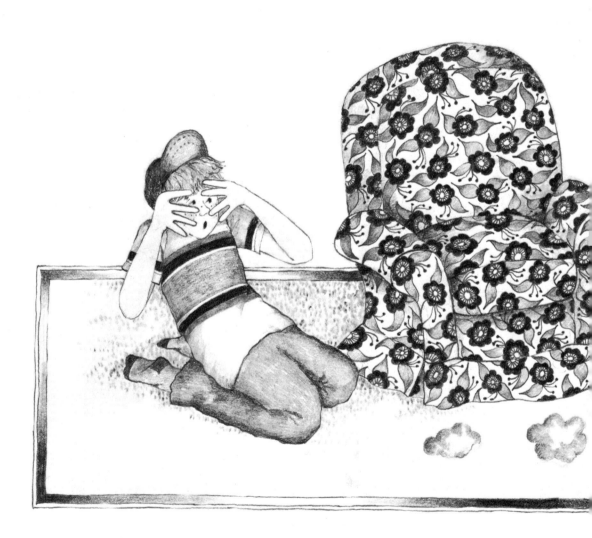

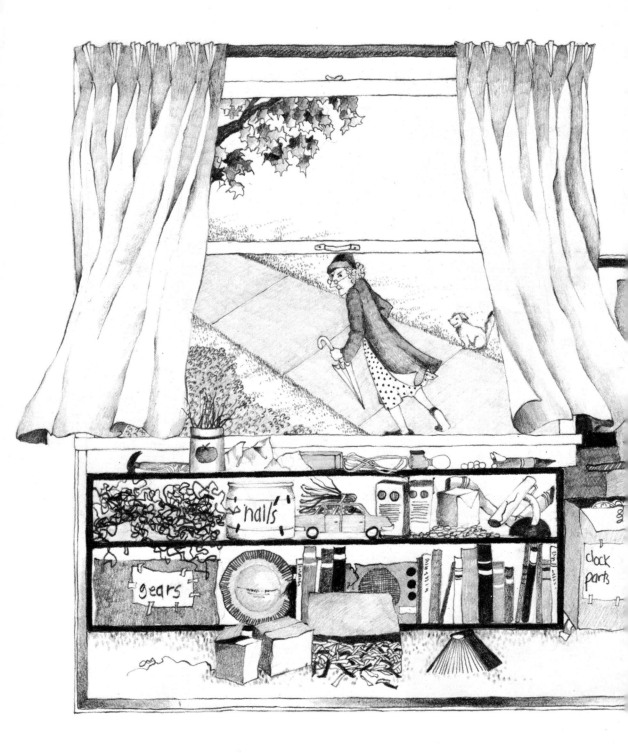

I also created a new breed of family pet, guaranteed not to shed or eat too much. It mostly rolled around the room going, "Squeak, squeak!" Our neighbor, Mrs. Loblaw, was at the house when I wound it up. When she heard it, she suddenly said she had to run.

One day I needed my skateboard. All the kids were going to Crandall Park. I was supposed to go too, but they got tired of waiting for me. It took three hours of digging before I finally uncovered my skateboard. It was in a box of "S" things with a Superman cape, metal springs and 23 shoelaces. When I got through looking, my room was in worse shape than before. Was I disgusted!

Another time I noticed a funny smell in my room.
The next day the smell was all over the hall, and by the
end of the week the whole house stank. It was sort of a

cross between sour milk and dinosaur breath, if you know what I mean. I was beginning to realize that my days as a great inventor were numbered.

Imagine how I felt when I came home from trash-picking one day and found a line of kids at the front door. My own kid brother, Alvie, was selling tickets for admittance to the World's Largest Indoor Dump. My room, of course.

My folks finally lost their patience. "Clear it up or clear out!" were their exact words.

I stalled and dilly-dallied. One day I could hardly open the door of my room. There was stuff piled up all over the place. I couldn't find my homework, which upset my teacher. I couldn't find any clean clothes, which upset my parents. But worst of all, I couldn't find the parts I needed for my inventions, which upset me! Even the dog had quit sleeping in my room because every time he swished his tail, ten things fell to the floor.

I realized that my parents were right. My collection of junk had to go. But where? And how?

Then it hit me. It would be the Sale of the Century . . . the Sale of Sales! Joe's Going Out of Business Sale! A garage sale was the perfect solution.

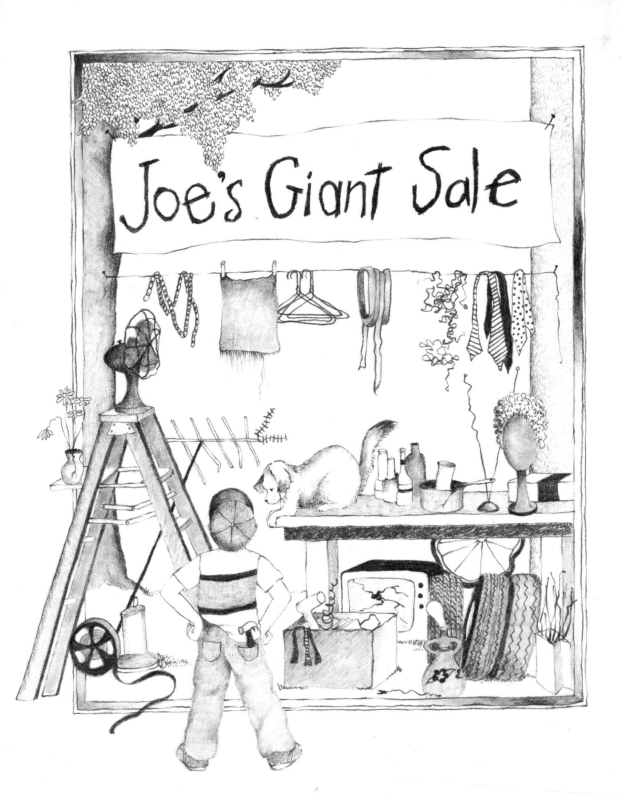

So I began to organize. And advertise. By the time the weekend rolled around I had the greatest bunch of bargains that I had ever seen. And believe me, I've seen quite a few!

I didn't attract the usual garage-sale customers. After all, I didn't have any baby furniture or toaster ovens. At first I found it hard to watch my one-of-a-kind treasures being carted off. But when I took a good look at my customers, I felt better. Many were pulling broken wagons, just like mine, and most of them had a faraway look in their eyes that I recognized. My junk was going to good homes, I could tell!

Well, I sold most of my terrific junk and left the rest for the garbage collector. By the end of the week I had a really creepy feeling when I went into my room. I mean, it was EMPTY!! So when I saw that broken typewriter in Mr. Murphy's trash, I knew just where to put it. Ditto for the garden hose and the furnace filters. And I have the best idea for another invention . . .

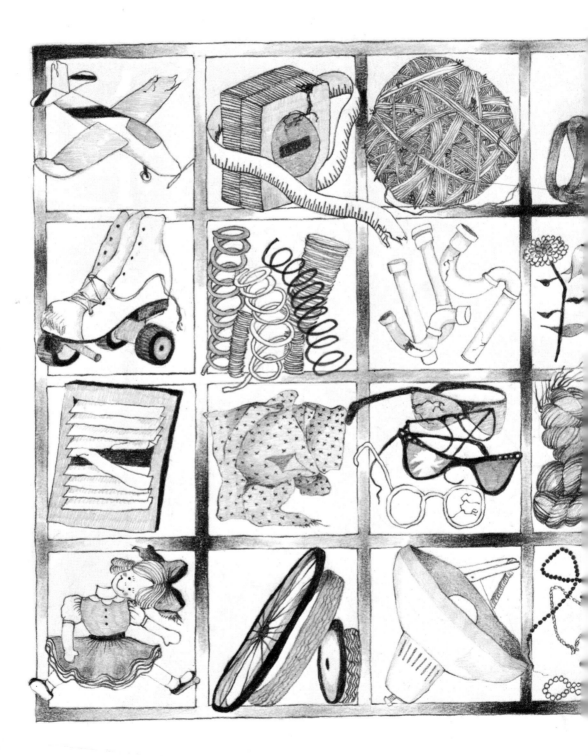

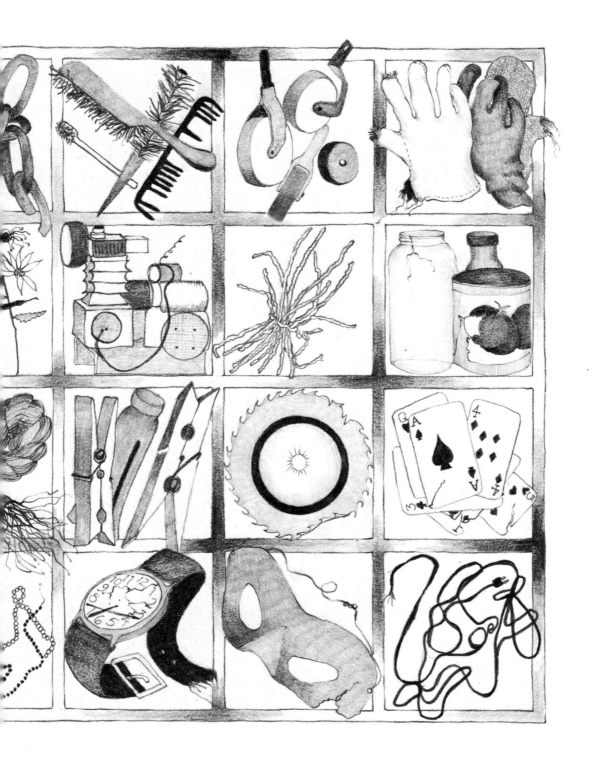